MW00876757

MaKaya's
New Friends

Mavis A. Johnson

To Blessini, my sweet Angel, with love!

In memory of my parents, Archie and Casceal Hayes!

Also, to my 1st and 2nd-grade students and my buddy John, my greatest supporters!

Thank you, guys!

One day, while sitting on her bed, 6-year-old MaKaya looked to the sky and wondered if Angels could give her new friends. MaKaya had been quarantined for 3 months. She had no friends around and couldn't go out to find them. A dangerous pandemic had spread across the land, and everyone had to stay home.

MaKaya was sad and tired of sitting in the house every day. She thought if her toys could talk, she would have friends again!

MaKaya's teacher told her to always wear her mask to stay safe. She wondered how a piece of paper knows what to do! MaKaya thought, "If I would pretend that the Angels could make my mask talk, then we could be friends and help each other out."

So, MaKaya used her imagination and called the Angels saying....
"Wonderful Angels in the sky; I hold my mask in my hand. Please make it talk to me if you can?"

"Marvelous Marvelous MasK, come to my face and do your tasK!"

STAY 6 feet away

Now do your part and stay six feet, and that sickness you will beat!

girLS!
"I'll do my part, wash my hands,
stay six feet away;
And the sicKness we will beat!"
6 feet

"Wear your mask,
stay six feet,
And the sickness
we will beat!
Wear your mask,
stay six feet,
And the sickness
we will beat!!"
MaKaya and her mask
chanted all through
the house.
"Oh, what fun we're
having," said MaKaya.
"Let's ask if all of my
toys can join us!"
"Hooray!" shouted
MaKaya's mask.

"Wonderful Angels in the sky, will you give all of my toys a try?" MaKaya pretended that the Angels had answered her request, so she went over to each of her toys and talked to them.

She went over to her stuffed animals.
"Freddy Teddy, big and strong,
stand my friend and come along!"

Silly Willy was brought
to life to sing and dance
with his dear wife.

The cat on the mat was really smitten to join the crew with all of her Kittens.

Bird in the cage was even happy to sing and share the stage.

The house was full of MaKaya's toys, marching and chanting...
"Wear your mask, stay six feet,
And the sickness, we will beat!!
Wear your mask, stay six feet,
And the sickness we will beat!!"

At the end of playtime,
MaKaya thanked all of her friends
and put them back.
"Marvelous mask and dear friends,
we had fun until the end.
I'll be back again and again!
Be safe, stay six feet,
and tomorrow we will meet!"

the end

MaKaya's New Friends
by Mavis A. Johnson

CPSIA information can be obtained
at www.ICGtesting.com
Printed in the USA
BVHW021056281021
620178BV00005B/121